For my bright,
beautiful niece Rosie
~ N.E.

For Rowan
& Magnus
~ H.T.

tiger tales
5 River Road, Suite 128, Wilton, CT 06897
Published in the United States 2022
Originally published in Great Britain 2021
by Caterpillar Books Ltd • Text by Nicola Edwards
Text copyright © 2021 Caterpillar Books Ltd.
Illustrations copyright © 2021 Hannah Tolson
ISBN-13: 978-1-68010-274-1 • ISBN-10: 1-68010-274-5
Printed in China • CPB/1600/2070/1221
2 4 6 8 10 9 7 5 3 1

www.tigertalesbooks.com

Look to the Skies

The yearly migration of the majestic monarch
butterfly across North America and back again
is a truly breathtaking, unique phenomenon.

This beautiful flight of bright, beating
wings unites young and old, rich and poor,
city-dwellers and country-folk, as people pause their
daily hustle and bustle and look up to see a
sky parade like no other on Earth.

tiger tales

We stop what we're doing and gaze at the skies;
we stand open-mouthed with the widest of eyes.

Our city is **bustling, busy,** and **bright,**
with so much to see, whether morning or night.

But when they appear, we just stop and stare;
they **flitter** and **flutter** like **jewels** in the air.

And then in the **hush** of the dusk come their **wings**.
Oh, **nature** is full of such **wonderful things**!

With days growing darker and winter ahead,
we kick **piles of leaves**, crispy brown, gold, and red.

Bright pumpkins are carved—they will soon come alive,
and it's time for the **orange parade** to arrive!

We love to play out in the glistening white **snow**,
but once the cold threatens, the **monarchs** must go.

They need the relief that the warmer south brings;
they all yearn to feel the **sun's rays** on their **wings**.

On our **wide, rolling plains,** we take in the view,
gazing up at the **heavenly** purple, pink, blue.

Our city is **colorful, friendly,** and **loud;**
it's **beautiful,** whether in sunshine or cloud.

But we're still in awe of the **monarch sky show.**
They've come a **long way**—not much farther to go.

The butterflies hustle and jostle for space—
a **butterfly blanket,** as each takes its place.

Three thousand miles is a valiant quest.
Now beneath the **blue skies**, our travelers **rest**.

They taught us all to look up to the skies.
There's **magic** around us. Just open your **eyes**.

The MONARCH BUTTERFLY

These butterflies are seeking warmer weather as they are not able to cope with frosty temperatures. They find their perfect microclimate in Mexico's ancient oyamel fir forests. These forests only exist at altitudes greater than 7,900 feet (2,400 m), and sadly, they are endangered, with only 2% of the original forests remaining.

It can take as many as five generations of monarchs, breeding en route, to complete the journey from the north to the south and back again. It's believed that the butterflies have a kind of built-in compass that allows them to sense the direction they need to travel, using the Earth's magnetic field.

Conservation of oyamel forests is essential to the future of monarchs as is the survival of the milkweed wildflower, which is the only thing monarch caterpillars eat. We need more people to grow milkweed for monarch butterflies to eat while they travel on their long journey.

Monarchs are found as far north as southern Canada, on both sides of the Rocky Mountains. The western monarchs will travel to central and southern California to spend the winter, while those that live east of the Rocky Mountains will migrate as far south as Mexico.